The Never Girls

before
the
bell

Written by
Kiki Thorpe

Illustrated by
Jana Christy

A STEPPING STONE BOOK™
RANDOM HOUSE 🏠 NEW YORK

For my sister, Elyse
—K.T.

For Will and Sadie xoxo
—J.C.

The author would like to thank Lindsey Brooks, Leah Weissinger, Darcie Birch, and Ms. Hertzberg's first graders for their thoughtful answers to her questions.

Library of Congress Cataloging-in-Publication Data
Thorpe, Kiki.
Before the bell / written by Kiki Thorpe ; illustrated by Jana Christy.
pages cm. — (Disney The Never girls ; 9)
"A Stepping Stone book."
Summary: "It's the first day of school, and Gabby can't wait to tell the fairies all about it. She even met a new friend who loves fairies as much as she does! But what will the Never Girls do when a fairy goes missing in Gabby's new classroom?"—
Provided by publisher.
ISBN 978-0-7364-3304-4 (paperback) — ISBN 978-0-7364-8167-0 (lib. bdg.) —
ISBN 978-0-7364-3305-1 (ebook)
[1. Fairies—Fiction. 2. Magic—Fiction. 3. First day of school—Fiction. 4. Schools—Fiction. 5. Friendship—Fiction.] I. Christy, Jana, illustrator. II. Disney Enterprises (1996–). III. Title.
PZ7.T3974Bef 2015
[Fic]—dc23
2014044460

randomhousekids.com/disney
Printed in the United States of America
10 9 8 7 6 5
This book has been officially leveled by using the F&P Text Level Gradient™ Leveling System.

Never Land

Far away from the world we know, on the distant seas of dreams, lies an island called Never Land. It is a place full of magic, where mermaids sing, fairies play, and children never grow up. Adventures happen every day, and anything is possible.

There are two ways to reach Never Land. One is to find the island yourself. The other is for it to find you. Finding Never Land on your own takes a lot of luck and a pinch of fairy dust. Even then, you will only find the island if it wants to be found.

Every once in a while, Never Land drifts close to our world . . . so close a fairy's laugh slips through. And every once in an even longer while, Never Land opens its doors to a special few. Believing in magic and fairies from the bottom of your heart can make the extraordinary happen. If you suddenly hear tiny bells or feel a sea breeze where there is no sea, pay careful attention. Never Land may be close by. You could find yourself there in the blink of an eye.

One day, four special girls came to Never Land in just this way. This is their story.

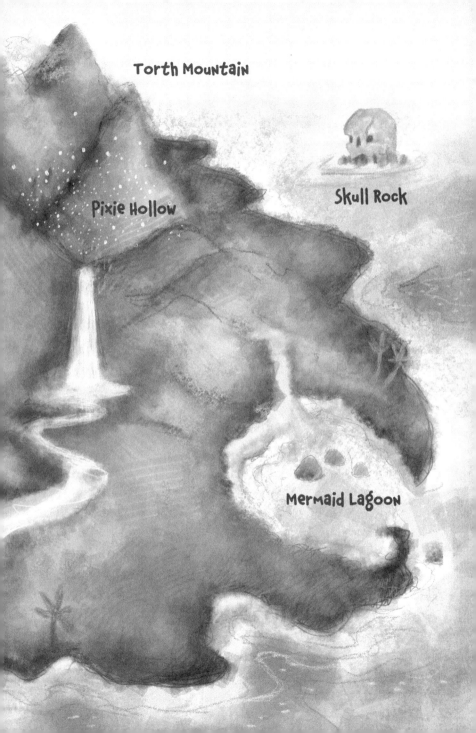

Chapter 1

"Okay, class. Get out your pencils. It's time to take a test," said Gabby Vasquez.

On the ground near her feet, four fairies sitting on snail shells picked up their hummingbird quills. "This is so exciting!" said the garden fairy Lily. "I've never taken a test before."

The light-talent fairy Iridessa looked worried. "Nobody said there'd be a test. I didn't study!" she whispered.

"Shh," said Gabby. "If you want to talk, you have to raise your hand, remember? Okay, the first question is, how many years old am I?"

Beck, an animal-talent fairy, scratched her head. "Do you mean in Clumsy years or mouse years?"

"Clumsy—I mean, *people* years," Gabby said.

The water fairy Silvermist tentatively raised a hand. "One hundred?" she guessed.

Gabby giggled. "No! I'm only six!"

Silvermist shrugged. "Well, I was close." One year and one hundred years weren't very different to fairies, who never grew older.

"Next question," Gabby said. "This time write down your answer. What's my favorite color?"

As the fairies bent over their toadstool
desks to write, Gabby heard someone say,
"That's an easy one. Pink!"

She looked up and saw a sparrow man
standing on a branch above her head.
Gabby knew most of the sparrow men in
Pixie Hollow, but she'd never seen this
one before. He wore an oak-leaf vest with
many patches. His hair stuck out every
which way from beneath his stocking cap.

And his shoes were so full of holes that Gabby could see his toes peeping out.

"Spinner's back!" Beck cried, jumping to her feet.

The sparrow man fluttered down, and the fairies surrounded him, welcoming him with smiles and hugs. Spinner returned their happy greetings, but his eyes kept traveling back to Gabby. "I hope you don't mind my saying so," he said at last, "but you're the biggest fairy I've ever seen."

"What? Oh!" Gabby laughed. He'd noticed her dress-up fairy wings! "I'm not a fairy. I'm a girl."

"She's an honorary fairy," said Iridessa.

Spinner looked impressed. "Well, I'll be jammed and jellied. You're the first honorary fairy I've met. What's your name?"

When Gabby told him, he chuckled. "I'm a bit 'gabby' myself. You and I will get along just fine."

"How did you know my favorite color was pink?" Gabby asked.

He shrugged and pointed to her pink tutu, pink T-shirt, and pink shoes. "Lucky guess."

"You've been gone a long time," Iridessa said to Spinner.

The sparrow man nodded. "A dozen moons at least. And I have as many stories to tell."

"Spinner is a story-talent fairy," Silvermist explained to Gabby. "He travels all over collecting tales. Then he brings them back to Pixie Hollow."

A story talent! Gabby had never met a story talent before. She squatted down to get a better look. "What kind of tales?" she asked him.

Spinner's eyes lit up. "Would you like to hear one?"

"Yes! Tell us a story!" the fairies all exclaimed. They sat down to listen. Gabby sat, too, wrapping her arms around her knees.

"It started one afternoon when I was in the forest eating Never Berries," Spinner began. "Now, as anyone who's ever had a Never Berry knows, there's nothing more delicious. Why, I'd say they taste just like a summer sunrise. . . ."

As he spoke, a strange thing happened. Gabby's mouth filled with a fresh, juicy taste, a flavor as sweet as strawberries and as bright as lemons. It was as if she were inside Spinner's story, eating berries right along with him.

"Before long I noticed a bird gobbling up the berries, too," Spinner went on. "He had an ivory beak and silver feathers. I knew he wasn't from Never Land."

Gabby could see the bird as clearly as if it were sitting next to her. Its white beak was stained with pink berry juice. Its feathers gleamed in the sunlight.

"I said to the bird, 'These berries are the finest food you'll ever taste.' But the bird puffed himself up and said, 'I've had better. Where I'm from, there's a cake as sweet and light as a dream. It's made from stardust and baked in moonlight.' Well, I knew I had to try that cake. So when the bird left, I hitched a ride. . . ."

Spinner kept talking, but Gabby no longer heard the words. She was suddenly in the story, riding on the silver bird's back. The bird's wings beat against the air as they rose up and up, flying through the day and into the night.

When they came out over the tops of the clouds, Gabby saw people there—tall men and women with moon-pale faces. They wore puffy white hats and stirred silver bowls filled with batter. A cloud kitchen! In one corner stood a white stone oven, arched like a half-moon. When it opened, Gabby caught a glimpse of cool blue light inside.

Nearby was a finished cake on an elegant silver stand. Its frosting looked as light and fluffy as the clouds. When the bird landed next to it, Gabby slid from

its back. The cake towered above her. She was tiny!

The bird snatched a bit of cake in its beak and gobbled it down. Gabby was reaching for a crumb when the cloud bakers noticed them. They rushed forward, waving their arms to drive the bird away. As they ran, the cloud rumbled with thunder. Lightning flashed beneath their feet. The bird flapped into the air, squawking. Gabby just managed to grab hold of its tail feather as it flew away.

But she couldn't hold on. The feather slipped from her grip and Gabby plummeted. . . .

Her wings! Gabby remembered to flutter them just in time. A moment later, she landed safely on the ground.

"And that's how I got back here,'
ner finished.

Gabby blinked. She was in Pixie Hollow, sitting on the ground with her arms
wrapped around her knees. Right where
she'd been the whole time.

"Wow," said a voice behind her. Gabby
turned and saw her older sister, Mia, and
Mia's best friends, Kate McCrady and
Lainey Winters. She had been so wrapped
up in Spinner's story, she hadn't heard
them approach.

"I've never heard a story like that," said
Mia.

"It was like I was right there in it,"
Lainey said. "I even had real wings."

Gabby nodded. That was exactly how
she'd felt.

"That's the storyteller's magic," Spinner said with a wink.

"But you know you can't believe a word of it," Beck said, laughing. "Tall tales are Spinner's specialty."

"You mean it's not true? It didn't really happen?" To think there was no such kitchen, no such bird, made Gabby's heart sink.

Spinner smiled gently. "Did it feel true to you?"

"Yes," Gabby admitted.

"Then that's what matters," Spinner said. "Now tell me *your* story. What's all this?" He motioned toward the toadstool desks and hummingbird quills.

"Gabby has been teaching us about school," Silvermist told him.

"The first day of school is tomorrow," Gabby said. "I was explaining how it works."

"As if you know," her older sister teased her. "You've only been to kindergarten."

"I do so know!" Gabby said. "Tomorrow I'll be in first grade. I know lots and lots about school. I know there's lunchtime and recess and story time—"

"Story time?" Spinner perked up.

"—and we learn about numbers and how to spell," Gabby went on. "And we get homework!"

The older girls laughed. "You think homework sounds fun?" said Kate.

Gabby nodded, hugging herself with

excitement. For years she'd watched her older sister heading off to school every day, then doing homework at the kitchen table and talking about her friends and all the important things she'd learned. Now it was finally going to be Gabby's turn. She couldn't wait to start first grade!

"But what's all this about story time?" Spinner asked.

"That's when the class reads a book together," Lainey explained. "Usually the teacher reads, but sometimes the kids read, too."

"Is that so? Hmm." Spinner looked thoughtful.

"Speaking of school, we were just coming to get you," Mia said to her sister. "It's time to go home. We have to get ready for tomorrow."

Gabby was always sorry to leave Pixie Hollow—the flowers, the Home Tree with its fascinating windows and rooms, and all her fairy friends. But she knew she'd be back. Gabby, Mia, and their friends had discovered a passage between the two worlds. They could visit anytime they liked, just by walking through Gabby's closet.

The girls said good-bye to the fairies, with promises to return as soon as they could. But when Gabby turned to say good-bye to Spinner, he had already disappeared.

"Oh well. Maybe I'll see him next time and he can tell me another story," Gabby said. Then she skipped off toward the fig tree, with the hole that led home.

Chapter 2

"Remember, don't turn the knob on the water fountain in the lunchroom too hard. It will squirt you in the face," Mia told Gabby. "And stay away from the left field at recess. That's where the big kids play kickball."

Gabby sighed. "And meet you right here on the front steps at the end of the day. I *know*, Mia." They'd already been over this on the walk to school.

Mia knelt and tied Gabby's shoe. Then

she untwisted the strap of Gabby's backpack. Gabby had left her fairy wings at home that day—they hadn't fit under the backpack. She'd thought she would miss them. But the bag filled the space on her back nicely, and it felt important in its own way.

"If you need anything, I'll be upstairs in Room 5B," Mia said. "Are you sure you don't want me to walk you to your classroom?"

"*Yesssss,*" Gabby said impatiently. *What is Mia so worried about?* she wondered. *First grade is going to be great!*

Other kids were arriving. Gabby spotted a few she knew from kindergarten. "Look, there's Lizzie!"

Mia turned to where she was pointing. "Lizzie?" she said, wrinkling her nose.

"You're not going to play with her again, are you?"

"Why not?" Gabby asked.

"Don't you remember last year in the park? She pushed you off the swing and you got a bloody nose," Mia reminded her.

"That was an accident," Gabby said. "We were trying to see if we could make the swing go all the way around the top."

"What about the time she broke the handles off all your china tea cups?" Mia asked.

"That was an accident, too," Gabby said.

"How can something that happens four times be an *accident*?" Mia asked. "I'm just saying that something bad seems to happen whenever you play with Lizzie."

"I *like* Lizzie," Gabby said. "She's fun,

and she's good at pretend games. Come on, I want to say hi."

Gabby took Mia's hand and dragged her over to where Lizzie was standing with her mother and her baby brother, Ollie. Gabby noticed that Lizzie had a fairy doll tucked under her arm. "Hi, Lizzie! I like your doll," she said.

"This is Glorinda," Lizzie said, holding her up so Gabby could see better. The doll had silky yellow hair, gold wings, and a fancy pink dress. "My grandma bought her for me. She cost twenty dollars."

"*Lizzie,*" her mother said. "That's not polite."

"But she did. And all Grandma bought for Ollie was a rattle." Lizzie looked pleased.

"She's really pretty," Gabby said, admiring the doll.

"You can hold her if you want," Lizzie offered.

Glorinda was much bigger than a real fairy, but Gabby thought she was lovely all the same. She liked every kind of fairy, real or not.

"Come on, Lizzie. Let's go meet your teacher," her mother said. "See you soon, Gabby."

Gabby handed the doll back. "See you inside," she said.

As Lizzie and her mother walked into the school, Gabby turned to her sister. "See? Lizzie is nice. She let me hold her doll."

"Well, just be careful," Mia said. "Oh, look, there's Kate." Mia and Kate were in the same class this year. "I'd better go. Don't forget, meet me right—"

"—here. I *know*, Mia."

"And, Gabby?" Mia lowered her voice. "Remember, Pixie Hollow is our secret, okay?"

Gabby nodded. As Mia went off to join the fifth graders, she hurried into her own classroom.

Her teacher, Ms. Jesser, was standing by the door, greeting the students as they arrived. "Find the desk with your name on it," Ms. Jesser said. "Then you can put your school supplies inside. When you're done your backpacks can be hung on the hooks."

All the desks had name tags shaped like fish. Gabby walked around until she found a pink starfish that said GABBY.

Her very own desk! It was in the first row, right next to the window. Gabby thought it was the best desk in the room.

As she reached into her backpack to take out her school supplies, her fingers touched something soft and warm. Gabby gasped and jerked her hand back. There was something alive in there!

Peering into the bag, she spied a familiar face. "Spinner!" Gabby whispered in surprise. "How did you get in there?"

"I used this thingamabob to open it. Right here, see?" Spinner pointed to the backpack's zipper. "Getting in was the easy part. But it only opens from one side. I thought I'd never get out!"

"That's not what I meant," Gabby whispered. "I meant, why aren't you in Pixie Hollow?"

"Oh, that." Spinner waved a hand. "When you left, I tagged along. I've never been to school before."

The boy at the desk next to Gabby's gave her a funny look. She realized it seemed as if she were talking to her backpack.

"I don't know," Gabby whispered to Spinner. "I might get in trouble." That summer, Gabby had brought the art fairy Bess to a wedding, and it had caused a lot of problems. She didn't want the same thing to happen on her first day of school.

"I'll keep out of the way," the sparrow man promised. "You won't even notice I'm here."

Gabby thought about it. It was too late to take Spinner back through the portal to Pixie Hollow. And besides, it would be fun to have a fairy at school.

"Okay," she whispered. "But you have to stay close to me. And don't let anyone see you."

"Don't worry," Spinner said. "I'm good at staying hidden."

Gabby held up her backpack and let Spinner fly into her desk. She hummed to herself as she put her school supplies in next to him. First grade was off to a good start, after all!

Chapter 3

"So this is a desk," Spinner said to himself. During his travels he'd hidden in many strange places. But he'd never been inside a school desk before. He strolled between Gabby's pencils and notebooks, taking it all in. One whole side of the desk was open, and Spinner had a nice view of the room when he looked out.

Class was getting started. "Welcome, everybody," the teacher said. "We're going to have so much fun this year. Now, how many of you are new at Evergreen Elementary? Hold up your hands."

A few kids raised their hands. Inside Gabby's desk, Spinner put his hand up, too.

Gabby giggled. "Spinner, the teacher can't see you," she whispered.

"But how am I going to learn anything if I don't follow along?" he said.

Ms. Jesser went over some classroom rules. Then she passed out sheets of paper to everyone.

"I thought we'd do something fun so I can get to know all of you," she said. "I want you each to draw a picture of YOU. Then write something about yourself. It can be anything—a sentence, or even just a word. Don't forget to put your name on your paper!"

The class got busy with their crayons and pencils. Spinner tried to wait patiently. But it was boring inside the desk. He wanted to do something, too.

Finally, he fluttered up and peeked over the edge of the desk. "Spinner, don't!" Gabby hissed. "Someone will see you." Quickly she leaned over, hiding him from the boy at the desk next to hers.

The sparrow man crouched behind Gabby's crayon box and glanced around. The other students had their heads down, drawing. The teacher was walking between the desks, looking at their work. But that didn't worry Spinner—he was invisible to grown-ups. Only children who believed in fairies would be able to see him.

"No one's looking. Let me see what you're doing," he said.

Gabby moved her hands so he could see her picture. She'd drawn herself in pink crayon, with brown hair and yellow wings. At the bottom of the paper, in darker pink, she'd written I LIKE FARYS.

"That's very fine indeed," Spinner said, nodding. "But it's missing something."

Spinner picked up a crayon and began to draw a tiny figure next to the drawing. The crayon was nearly as tall as he was. It took a lot of effort to move it. He drew in silver wings and added a smudge of gold for a fairy glow.

"It's you!" Gabby whispered.

Spinner nodded, puffing out his chest a little. He took a leaf-kerchief from the pocket of his vest and mopped his brow.

"I didn't know school would be so much work," he said.

"You're supposed to write something, too," Gabby reminded him.

"That's right." Spinner tried to pick up Gabby's pencil. But he could only lift it halfway. As he struggled to balance it, the pencil slipped from his grip and rolled off the desk.

At that moment, Ms. Jesser walked

past. "Here you go, Gabby," she said. She picked up the pencil and placed it on the desk, right at Spinner's feet.

Gabby froze, looking up at the teacher in alarm.

Ms. Jesser smiled. "It's okay," she said. "It's only a pencil. Happens all the time." Then she walked on to the next desk.

Spinner chuckled. "She can't see me, remember?" he whispered. "Now help me with this thing."

While Gabby held the pencil, Spinner guided the tip. Next to his drawing he wrote:

Small feller,
storyteller

When everyone had handed in their drawings, Ms. Jesser took the students on a tour of the classroom. She showed them the art supplies and the water fountain. She showed them the pencil sharpener that cranked around and around. And she showed them the big round blue carpet, where they would sit for story time.

"When *is* story time?" Spinner piped up. He was peeking out from the front pocket of Gabby's dress.

"Shh," Gabby whispered. She gently poked him down again, tucking him out of sight.

"And this is *my* favorite part of our room," Ms. Jesser said as she led the class to the back corner. "Our classroom library."

Spinner carefully raised his head and peeped over the edge of the pocket. He saw a long bookshelf stuffed with books. Narrow books, fat books, tall books, short books, books with brightly colored

covers—to the sparrow man they seemed to stretch on for miles.

Spinner himself kept all his stories in his head. But he knew Clumsies liked to write theirs down. If he could just get to that bookshelf, Spinner knew he'd have all the stories his noggin could hold!

Suddenly a bell rang, so loud it made Spinner's teeth rattle. The kids collected their lunch boxes and schoolbags and lined up at the door.

"What's going on?" Spinner whispered to Gabby.

"It's time for the best part of the day," Gabby replied.

"Story time?" Spinner asked.

"No," Gabby told him. "Lunch!"

Chapter 4

The school cafeteria was filled with noise. Gabby sat at a long table with the other first graders. Lizzie sat across from her, with Glorinda by her side. Every now and then, Lizzie pretended to feed the doll a bite.

"Guess what? I think I saw a real fairy," Lizzie told Gabby.

Gabby swallowed her bite of sandwich with a gulp. "You did? Where?"

"In my backyard," Lizzie said in a

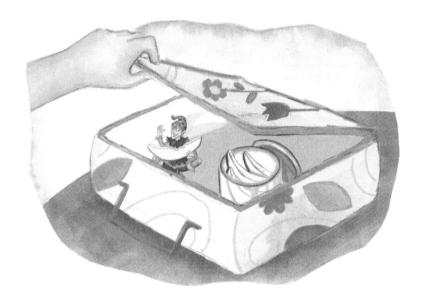

hushed voice. "I saw something *glowing*.
But when I looked again, it was gone. My
mom said it was probably just a firefly.
But I'm sure it was a fairy."

"Oh." Gabby sighed in relief. Her Spinner secret was still safe. She was bursting
to show him to Lizzie. But she remembered Mia's warning not to tell anyone
about Pixie Hollow.

Gabby lifted the lid on her lunch box and peeked inside. Spinner was sitting in the corner, munching on an apple slice. He held it with both hands and took bites out of the middle, as if it were a slice of watermelon. When he saw Gabby, he waved.

"Why do you keep doing that?" Lizzie asked.

Gabby closed the lid with a snap. "Doing what?"

"Looking inside your lunch box."

"I'm just looking is all," Gabby said.

"Well, I want to go out and play," Lizzie said. She crumpled up the remains of her food and stuffed them in her lunch bag. Then she grabbed Glorinda. "Come on!"

Gabby finished the last bite of her sandwich. Then she carried her lunch box to the cubbies that the lunchroom monitor had showed them. When she was sure no one was looking, she carefully transferred Spinner into the pocket of her dress.

"Are you okay?" she whispered.

"Snug as a joey in a kangaroo's pocket," Spinner whispered back.

"Hurry up, Gabby!" Lizzie was already at the door.

Outside in the schoolyard kids were jumping rope, swinging from the monkey bars, and bouncing balls off the side of the school building.

"Let's go over there," Lizzie said. She pointed to a part of the lawn that was covered in dandelions.

When they got there, Lizzie plopped down in the grass. "Let's pretend this is a magical place where fairies live."

"Yeah!" said Gabby. "We can call it Pixie Hollow."

Inside her pocket, Spinner laughed.

Lizzie looked around. "Did you hear something?"

"No," said Gabby, squirming a little. Keeping a secret was so hard!

"Let's make a picnic for Glorinda," Lizzie suggested, setting the doll down. She placed a leaf in front of Glorinda. "This can be the picnic blanket."

Gabby pulled up a handful of grass and piled it on the leaf. "This is the salad."

Lizzie plucked dandelions. "These are the cakes. Glorinda just *adores* dandelion cake."

Spinner chuckled again.

"There it is again!" Lizzie cried. "It sounds like little bells. Don't you hear it?"

Gabby shook her head, but she was starting to giggle. She clapped both her hands over her mouth. But the secret came bursting out anyway. "I have a fairy!" she exclaimed.

"What?" Lizzie stared at her.

"He's a sparrow man, actually. His name's Spinner, and he came to school today in my backpack." Once she'd started talking, the secret came out in a rush, like a breath of air she'd been holding for too long.

Gabby held open her pocket. "Come out, Spinner. Meet my friend."

When Spinner flew out of her pocket, Lizzie's eyes opened so wide that Gabby thought they might pop right out of her

head. Spinner hovered in the air between the girls. When he tipped his cap to Lizzie, she squealed.

"Where did you get him?" she whispered to Gabby.

"He came from Pixie Hollow," Gabby said.

"Can I hold him?" Lizzie asked.

"It's up to Spinner," Gabby told her. When he nodded, Lizzie held out her hand and Spinner landed lightly on her palm.

"It tickles!" Lizzie said, giggling.

Gabby laughed, too. "I know!"

As Lizzie bent closer to look at Spinner, the bell rang. Gabby knew that meant recess was over. "Give him here," she said, reaching for the sparrow man.

But Lizzie jerked back. She put her

other hand over him so he couldn't fly away. "Not yet!" she said. "I want to hold him a little longer."

Gabby could see the rest of their class lining up by the door to go inside. "Come on, we're going to be late," she said.

"I just want to borrow him for a little bit," Lizzie said. "I let you hold Glorinda, didn't I?"

"Give him back, Lizzie!" Gabby grabbed for Spinner. But Lizzie held him out of her reach. From inside Lizzie's hands, Gabby heard Spinner cry out.

"Stop! You're hurting him!" Gabby yelled.

Lizzie gasped and opened her hands. Spinner shot out at once. He flew straight to Gabby.

"See? He's okay," Lizzie said.

The sparrow man wasn't hurt, but he looked a little dazed. Gabby placed him gently in her pocket. Then, keeping her hand over him, she stood and joined the rest of the class.

Lizzie followed. "Don't be mad, Gabby," she said. "I just wanted to see him. Can you bring me a fairy, too?"

"No!" Gabby whispered. "And don't talk so loud. It's a secret." She was starting to feel sorry she'd said anything to Lizzie at all.

On the way back to the classroom, Gabby kept her hand over her pocket. She didn't want to take any more chances. *From now on, I'll be extra careful,* she told herself. She was relieved when they got to the classroom and Spinner was safe inside her desk again.

Chapter 5

Spinner was not glad to be inside Gabby's desk again. He sat on a pink rubber eraser with his chin in his hands. Out in the classroom, the students were playing a game to remember each other's names. But Spinner didn't feel like following along.

School wasn't turning out to be quite the adventure he had hoped. It was all "line up here" and "sit down there" and rules, rules, rules. Spinner liked to roam and explore—that was how he found the best stories! The desk's metal walls were beginning to feel like a cage. But Spinner knew he couldn't wander where the other kids could see him. Meeting Lizzie had taught him that much.

As he gazed out at the classroom, Spinner's eyes fell on the bookshelf in the back. *A whole treasure trove of stories just sitting there,* he thought. *What a shame.*

Then again . . .

Why should I stay here twiddling my thumbs? I've crossed rivers before. I've crossed oceans! How hard could it be to cross a Clumsy classroom?

Spinner crept to the edge of the desk and looked down. It was a long way to the floor. Normally he could have flown, but he knew fluttering his wings would attract attention.

He dangled his feet over the edge and eased himself onto a desk leg. *Squeeeeee!* Spinner's hands squeaked against the metal as he slid down. He darted a glance at Gabby. But she was caught up in the game and didn't notice.

On the floor, Spinner hid behind a leg of Gabby's chair, plotting his next move.

There were four desks between him and his goal—and twenty-four sets of eyes that might spot him. Spinner wished he could put out his glow. It was hard to be invisible when you glimmered.

Taking a deep breath, Spinner dashed to the next desk. He reached the front leg and dove behind it.

He waited, his heart pounding. But the class went right on playing their game. No one had noticed him.

Spinner walked beneath the desk, skirting a boy's sneakers. As he passed under the chair, Spinner felt a prickling along his spine—that always signaled danger.

He looked up and froze. A hand was coming toward him! He'd been spotted!

But the hand passed right by him. The

boy scratched his ankle, then straightened up again.

"Whew!" Spinner's breath whooshed out in relief.

When he felt it was safe, Spinner darted to the next desk. He paused behind a chair leg to let his knees stop shaking. Fairies and sparrow men usually fluttered their wings, even when they walked. It helped them keep their balance. But to avoid attracting attention, Spinner had kept his wings folded. It made running a lot harder.

As he rested, the chair leg he was hiding behind suddenly rose into the air. Spinner looked up as the girl above him tipped back, back, back. Her chair balanced precariously on its two rear legs.

The teacher said something, and suddenly the chair came crashing back down. Spinner leaped out of the way to avoid being pinned beneath the falling leg.

He pulled a leaf-kerchief from his pocket and mopped his brow. *Only two more desks to go,* he thought.

He reached the next desk without trouble. But when he got to the fourth, he realized he had a problem. Between him and the library there was a wide-open stretch of floor. How was he going to cross *that* without being seen?

Spinner sighed. There was only one thing to do, and it wasn't going to be pretty.

Getting down on his hands and knees, Spinner folded his wings over his back. He pulled his cap down low on his head and dimmed his glow as much as possible.

Then, feeling very silly, he scuttled across the floor like a cockroach. If anyone spotted him, he hoped they'd mistake him for a giant water bug.

When he reached the corner, Spinner dove behind a huge beanbag chair. He looked back at the classroom. All the children were facing the front of the room, away from him. He was safe now. Spinner hopped to his feet and dusted himself off. He wasn't a proud fellow, but it was undignified to act like a bug. *When I tell this story back in Pixie Hollow, perhaps I'll leave that part out,* he thought.

The bookshelf loomed before him, full of hidden treasure. Spinner rubbed his hands together. "Now to find some stories!"

Chapter 6

Spinner strolled along the bottom shelf, gazing up at the books. They towered above him, so high that he had to crane his neck to read the words written on their spines.

"'Di-no-saurs,'" he read, pausing in front of a particularly fat book. "I wonder what this is about?"

Spinner gripped the top edge of the book and tried to pull it down. But the book was wedged in tightly. He fluttered his wings hard, but it wouldn't budge.

On the floor next to the bottom of the shelf, Spinner spied a pencil. That might do the trick! He hoisted it up, balancing it on both shoulders to carry it.

Spinner darted a glance at the class. They were all still caught up in their game. And he was well hidden behind the giant beanbag chair. Unless someone passed by the bookshelf, they wouldn't see him.

Bracing the round eraser end against the top edge of the book, Spinner levered it out of the shelf.

Slowly the book began to tip. Then it toppled like a falling tree and fell open onto the floor.

"Ahhh!" Spinner leaped back as a huge lizard sprang from the pages. He dove into

the empty gap in the bookshelf and huddled there, trembling.

A lizard inside a book? he thought. *How can that be?*

"Maybe it's a magic book!" There were books like that in Pixie Hollow, ones where ice formed on the pages or wind blew the words around. But Spinner had never seen one with animals inside.

He had to take another look.

Holding the pointed end of the pencil out like a spear, Spinner peeked out from the bookshelf. The lizard was right where he'd left it, standing atop the open book. Its jaws were open wide in a silent roar.

"Well, I'll be picked and pickled," Spinner said to himself. "It's made out of paper!" He read the words printed next to it. *"Tyrannosaurus rex."*

Spinner shuddered. "I think I'd like a book with a few less teeth," he said, hefting it closed.

A ways down the shelf, another title caught Spinner's eye—*Fairy Tales.* "What could that be about?" he wondered.

This book was easier to remove. Spinner was able to pull it out with just his bare hands. He slid it to the floor, using a bit of fairy dust to make it lighter.

The book fell open to a picture of a tiny girl riding on the back of a bird. Spinner read the words beneath the picture. "'Thumbelina'? I know that story!"

Spinner began to read, walking back and forth along the page. The words were so big that it took him several strides to reach the end of each sentence.

"Thumbelina" was the story of a tiny girl no bigger than her mother's thumb. She was stolen from her home by a toad who wanted Thumbelina to marry her son.

"But they've got the story all wrong!" Spinner exclaimed. "Every soul in Never Land knows Thumbelina was a fairy, not a girl! And a toad didn't steal her— a Clumsy did! Imagine a toad wanting to

marry a fairy!" Spinner laughed so hard he had to stop and wipe his eyes with his leaf-kerchief. "Leave it to the Clumsies to get everything backward!"

Spinner went on reading, pausing every now and then to chuckle or shake his head. He didn't notice that the class had stopped playing their game.

A prickle crept up the back of his neck. But Spinner thought it was just the excitement of the story.

The prickle grew stronger—so strong Spinner could feel it in his toes. Only then did he think to look up.

But he was too late. All Spinner saw was a flash of pale hands. Then the book closed around him with a *snap*.

Chapter 7

"Spinner, wake up. It's story time," Gabby whispered. The sparrow man had been quiet for so long, she guessed he must have fallen asleep.

"Spinner?" Gabby whispered again. She leaned down to look inside her desk. Why couldn't she see his glow?

Gabby moved her box of crayons, hoping he was behind it. No Spinner. She looked behind her math book. She even checked inside her pencil box. But the sparrow man was gone.

Gabby got a funny feeling in her stomach. Where could Spinner be? And how could he have gone anywhere without her seeing?

Other first graders were gathering on the big round carpet, waiting for story time to start. "As soon as *everyone* is sitting, I can read the story," Ms. Jesser said, looking at Gabby.

Gabby went to the circle and sat down. But she kept an eye out for Spinner. He had waited all day to hear a story. He wouldn't miss it now, would he?

The teacher began to read a book about a little bear on his first day of school. But Gabby couldn't pay attention. Her eyes

roamed the classroom. There! That gleam of light by the window—was it Spinner's glow?

No, it was only sunlight reflecting off a pair of scissors. A second later, Gabby gave a little jump. A tiny face was smiling out from the teacher's desk! Gabby squinted, then sighed. It was just a picture on the side of a coffee cup.

"Some people seem to have the wiggles," Ms. Jesser said, interrupting her reading. "*Everyone* needs to have their eyes on me." She was looking at Gabby again.

Gabby felt her face turn red. Now Spinner had gotten her in trouble with the teacher, too!

After that, she tried to pay attention. But as the day went on, she started to worry. What could have happened?

When the last bell rang, there was still no sign of Spinner. As the other kids got their backpacks and left, Gabby didn't know what to do. What if he came back looking for her and she wasn't there?

Gabby saw Lizzie getting ready to leave. "Lizzie, I can't find Spinner anywhere!" she whispered.

Lizzie gave her a funny look. "I have to go," she said. "I forgot I have to help my mom today." She grabbed her backpack and hurried out the door.

I guess she's still mad at me, Gabby thought with a sigh.

Finally, she and Ms. Jesser were the only ones left in the classroom. "Are you waiting for someone, Gabby?" the teacher asked.

Gabby nodded. Then, thinking better

of it, she shook her head. She was afraid the teacher might ask who she was waiting for.

Ms. Jesser gave her a confused smile. "Is someone coming to pick you up?" she tried again.

"Oh!" Gabby suddenly remembered that Mia was waiting for her. Mia would know what to do! "I gotta go. Bye, Ms. Jesser," she said, hurrying away.

In the hallway, she almost bumped into Mia, Kate, and Lainey.

"Where have you been?" Mia exclaimed. "We've been waiting forever. . . . What's wrong?" she asked when she noticed Gabby's expression.

"Um, don't be mad," Gabby said.

Mia frowned. "Uh-oh. Don't be mad about *what*, Gabby?"

Gabby took a deep breath. "Spinner's missing . . . but it's not my fault," she added quickly.

"Spinner the sparrow man?" asked Kate. "What do you mean he's missing? Missing from *where*?"

Gabby explained how Spinner had hidden in her backpack so he could hear the stories at school. "And once he was here, I couldn't take him home. So I put him in my desk. I told him to stay there. But then he disappeared!"

Mia rubbed her forehead. "Gabby, this is even worse than when you took Bess to the wedding!"

"It's not Gabby's fault," Kate pointed out. "She didn't ask Spinner to come. I wish he'd stowed away in *my* backpack. It would have made school a lot more interesting today."

"Don't worry, we'll help you find him," Lainey said, putting her arm around the little girl.

"Let's start by checking your classroom, since that's the last place you saw him," Kate suggested.

When they got back to Gabby's classroom, the door was closed and the lights were off. "Are we going to get in trouble?" Gabby asked as they went into the empty room.

"If anyone asks, we'll just tell them we're looking for something we lost," Mia said. "Which is the truth."

Kate got down on her knees and peered inside Gabby's desk.

"Why are you looking in there?" Gabby asked. "I know he's not there."

"You always start searching for clues at the scene of the crime," Kate said. "At least, that's how the detectives on TV do it."

"What crime?" Mia asked. "For all we know, Spinner just flew away on his own."

"I know," Kate said. "But it's more exciting if there was a crime."

Lainey was at the back of the room, exploring near the bookshelves. "Look!" she said suddenly. She pointed to a pencil on the floor.

"It's a pencil. So what?" Kate said.

"It's *sparkly*," Lainey said. The other girls looked closer. Now they saw that the side of the pencil glittered faintly.

"Fairy dust!" Gabby whispered.

"Our first clue!" Kate exclaimed. "Good work, Lainey."

"Maybe Spinner left a trail that we can follow," Mia said.

The girls searched the rest of the classroom. But they didn't find any more fairy dust. "It's like he vanished into thin air," Lainey said.

"The trail has gone cold," Kate agreed, furrowing her brow.

"He could be anywhere," Mia said. "Maybe he's just off exploring. He'll probably turn up tomorrow," she reassured her sister.

Gabby nodded, but she didn't feel much better. What if Spinner *didn't* turn up? As they went to leave, Mia suddenly said, "What's that sticking out of your backpack, Gabby?"

A bit of yellow hair was poking out of the zipper. Gabby opened the bag and pulled out Glorinda. "It's Lizzie's doll," she said. "But *I* didn't put her in here. I wonder why Lizzie left her?"

 The older girls looked at each other. "Gabby, you didn't by any chance tell Lizzie about

Spinner, did you?" Mia asked.

"Maybe," Gabby admitted. "But she loves fairies. She'd never tell. When you said not to talk about Pixie Hollow to anyone, I didn't think you meant Lizzie."

Mia rolled her eyes. "I *especially* meant Lizzie."

Lainey picked up Glorinda. "Well, I think we may have found the clue we were looking for."

Kate grinned. "The trail is hot again. And we're on the case!"

Chapter 8

For the second time that day, Spinner was getting a close look at the inside of a backpack. It wasn't Gabby's this time—this one was purple instead of blue. But one thing was the same. Both bags opened only one way—from the outside. Try as he might, Spinner couldn't find a way out.

And he had another, bigger problem—he couldn't fly. One wing had been bent when the book closed on him. Spinner gave it a flap, testing it, but he knew it was useless. A healing-talent fairy could straighten it out. But of course, there were no healing fairies around.

"You're in a pretty pickle this time," Spinner said to himself. He wasn't too troubled, though. He'd been in plenty of pickles before. They usually made for very good stories.

The worst part was that it was *boring* inside the backpack. Whoever had nabbed him hadn't even been thoughtful enough to drop the book in with him. "And I'd just gotten to the good part," Spinner said.

He made himself comfortable on a small pack of tissues. Then, with nothing else to do, he began to tell himself a story. "So there I was, reading a book and minding my own business. When out of nowhere, someone came along—"

Spinner paused. "Someone" wasn't very good, he thought. No, it wasn't good at all. Who wanted to hear a story about "someone"?

He tried again. "A villain came along. . . ." That was a little better.

"A *bandit* came along—no, *three* bandits! Yes, much better! Three bandits with gold teeth and red eyes came along. They snapped me up in the book and took me off to their hideout. . . ."

Suddenly, the backpack gave a lurch. Spinner fell from his seat as the bag was lifted into the air. He was moving! He tried to peer out the crack at the bottom of the zipper. But he couldn't see anything through the tiny hole.

"You there! Let me out!" he called. But if anyone heard him, they didn't answer.

The light coming through the fabric grew brighter for a time, then dimmed. Spinner could tell that they had gone outside, then indoors again. But indoors where?

There came another bump as the backpack was set down. The zipper slowly began to peel back. Spinner steeled himself to face his fairy-napper.

A round, freckled face peered down at him. *It isn't a bandit after all,* Spinner thought with a twinge of disappointment. It was Gabby's friend Lizzie.

"Hi, little fairy," Lizzie whispered. "We're home."

Her big hands reached for him. Spinner braced

himself as she lifted him into the air.

The girl held him up to her face, so close that he could have counted each and every one of her freckles. Spinner had never been this close to a Clumsy's face before. He noticed her long eyelashes and the fine hairs that covered her cheeks like fuzz on a peach.

Lizzie was studying him, too. Her giant eyes roamed from the toes of his holey shoes up to the tip of his stocking cap. "I can't believe it," she whispered. "A *real* fairy."

"I'm a sparrow man, technically," Spinner said.

At the sound of his voice, Lizzie gave an excited squeak and almost dropped him. Spinner grabbed her thumb to keep from falling.

"Steady now. It's a long way down," he said.

"Sorry." She lowered him to the floor. As he stepped off her hand, he sank up to his ankles in the carpet. Looking around, Spinner saw he was in a bedroom. The cliff next to Lizzie was a bed. A blue coverlet spilled over its side. Beyond it, Spinner could see the looming shape of a dresser.

Lizzie watched him the whole time. She seemed to be waiting for him to do something. "Why don't you fly?" she asked at last.

"I can't. My wing is bent. *Somebody* closed it in a book," Spinner said.

"Sorry," the girl said again, and this time she really did look sorry. "I was afraid you'd try to fly away." She leaned closer to examine the damaged wing. "Does it hurt?"

"Not really." Fairy wings were like hair or fingernails—they didn't feel pain.

"So does that mean I can still have my wish?" Lizzie asked.

"What wish?" asked Spinner.

"The wish that you're going to grant me."

Spinner chuckled to himself. The Clumsies he'd met in his travels always asked for wishes. Somehow, they'd all gotten the idea that fairies lived to grant them. *From those silly fairy tales, no doubt,* Spinner thought.

"I can't grant wishes. I'm not that kind of magic folk," he told Lizzie. "But if you were going to ask for a wish, what would you wish for?"

"I want to *be* a fairy!" Lizzie exclaimed. "I want to be tiny and take rides on birds and wear dresses made out of flowers."

She looked at Spinner hopefully. He shook his head.

"Well, if you can't fly and you can't grant wishes, what *can* you do?" Lizzie asked with a sigh.

"I can tell you a story," he said, then wished he hadn't. Storytelling was his magic. He didn't share it with just anyone.

But Lizzie didn't seem to be listening. "Oh! I almost forgot!" she said, giving a little jump. She grabbed Spinner and whisked him through the air with a speed that took his breath away.

"You have to warn me when you're going to pick me up," he said, gasping.

"Sorry," Lizzie said again as she set him

down on top of the dresser. "I wanted you to see my fairy house."

Standing on the dresser was a little round hut. It was made out of glued-together twigs and bits of moss. A path of seashells led up to the front door.

"Go on. Go inside!" Lizzie urged.

Spinner opened the door. In the room was a fairy-sized bed and a small table. The table was set with a plate, bowl, and cup, as if waiting for a guest.

"It's very nice," Spinner said uneasily.

"It's your new home!" Lizzie said. "I made it myself. I was going to put it outside so a fairy would come and live in it. But now you're here! I've always wanted to have a fairy."

For the first time that day, Spinner started to feel worried. "But I can't stay,"

he tried to explain. "I already have a home in Pixie Hollow."

Lizzie's expression clouded. "You *have* to stay!" she cried, her voice rising to a frightening pitch that filled the room. "You haven't even done any magic yet. And besides, I traded Gabby fair and square."

Traded? thought Spinner. What was Lizzie talking about?

The door to the bedroom opened and a woman came in. She had the same green eyes and freckles as Lizzie. She was holding a baby on her hip.

"Lizzie?" she said. "Please keep your voice down. Ollie's trying to nap."

"Mommy, look!" Lizzie cried. Without warning, she scooped Spinner off the dresser and held him up.

From the way she looked right past him, Spinner could tell that Lizzie's mother couldn't see him. But the baby could. He gurgled with delight and shot out his chubby hands.

"Ollie, no!" Lizzie screeched and jerked Spinner out of his reach.

"Lizzie!" her mother said. "Please don't scream at the baby. What's gotten into you?"

"But he almost got my fairy!"

"What fairy?" her mother asked, frowning.

"He's *right here!*" Lizzie waved Spinner under her mother's nose. Spinner clung to her hand, trying not to fall. "His name's Spinner. I traded Glorinda for him at school—"

"Glorinda?" her mother interrupted. "That nice doll Grandma bought you? You shouldn't have done that. What are we going to tell Grandma?"

"But, *Mom!* I have a *real* fairy now," Lizzie tried to explain.

Her mother rubbed her forehead in a tired way. "When you go to school tomorrow, ask for your doll back. And please try to be quiet this afternoon. Ollie really needs to sleep."

She turned and left, with the baby looking back over her shoulder at Spinner and Lizzie.

When they were gone, Lizzie flopped onto the bed. She set Spinner down on the pillow next to her, to his great relief.

"It's not fair," Lizzie cried. "All she cares about is Ollie. She doesn't even care that *I* have a fairy. She pretended she didn't even see you!"

"She can't see me," Spinner explained. "Most grown-ups can't."

"Why not?" Lizzie asked with a sniffle.

"Only those who believe in fairies can see them."

Lizzie considered this. "Having a fairy is nothing like I thought it would be," she said with a sigh.

She looked so sad that Spinner couldn't help feeling a little sorry for her. "So will you take me back to Gabby now?" he asked gently.

Lizzie frowned. "Why should Gabby have a fairy and not me?" she asked.

Lizzie thought fairies were like dolls, Spinner realized. Something to keep for your own or trade away. He had to make her understand that he didn't belong to anyone.

Suddenly, he thought of a way he could. It was so clear to him, he wondered why he hadn't thought of it before. "Lizzie, maybe I can make your wish come true after all," he said.

Lizzie's eyes went round. "You *can?*"

Spinner nodded. "I'm going to tell you a

story. It's called 'Thumbelina.'"

"Oh." Lizzie's face fell. "I thought you meant you could make me into a fairy. Anyway, I already know that story. My mom read it to me."

"Ah," said Spinner. "But you've never heard *me* tell it. Now listen. . . ."

Chapter 9

Gabby stood on the steps of Lizzie's house, staring up at her front door. The door was red with a little metal knocker. Next to the door was a doorbell. Gabby glanced from the doorbell to the knocker. Which one was she supposed to use?

She looked back at Mia, Kate, and Lainey, who were watching from the sidewalk. Mia made a little motion with her hands as if to say "get on with it."

Gabby took a breath and rang the bell. Then, for good measure, she rapped the doorknocker, too.

She could hear a baby crying inside the house. "Coming!" someone shouted.

After a long wait, the door opened. But it wasn't Lizzie standing there. It was her mother. She was holding Lizzie's crying baby brother, and she looked annoyed.

"What is it?" she said. Then she saw Gabby. "Oh. Lizzie can't play right now, Gabby. Ollie is having trouble napping. Every little thing keeps waking him up. So we can't have anyone over today." She jiggled the baby on her hip.

Gabby's feet felt frozen to the step. She knew she should say something about Spinner. But the way Lizzie's mom was looking at her made her mind go blank.

"We'll make a playdate for another time, okay?"

"Okay," said Gabby.

"Bye." Lizzie's mother went inside and closed the door. Gabby turned and walked back down the steps to where Mia, Kate, and Lainey were waiting.

"What happened?" asked Kate.

"Lizzie's mom says she can't play," Gabby told them.

"That's it?" Mia rolled her eyes. "Gabby, why didn't you ask her if Lizzie could come *out*?"

"Or you could have told her she has something that belongs to you and you need it back," said Lainey.

"I didn't think of that." Gabby felt close

to crying again. "You guys should have come with me."

"It's okay," Kate said. "I think I have another idea. Come on."

Kate led them around to the side of Lizzie's house. A thick hedge grew along the wall. Kate squeezed between the wall and the hedge, then motioned for the other girls to follow.

"What are we doing?" Mia whispered.

"We'll just look in the window and find out where Spinner is. Then we can figure out how to rescue him," Kate said. "Come on."

They edged along the side of the house. The hedge scratched Gabby's arms and snagged her shirt. When they reached a window, Kate, who was tallest, stood on her tiptoes to look inside. But she could just barely peek over the windowsill.

"I can't see much. Come here, Gabby. We'll boost you up," she said.

Kate grabbed Gabby around the waist. Mia and Lainey helped lift, until Gabby's head was just above the window-sill. Through the window, Gabby could see Lizzie's little brother Ollie. He was

standing up in his crib, crying. But when he saw Gabby, he stopped.

Gabby waved at him. Then she made a funny face. Ollie stared at her, drooling a little.

"Do you see Spinner?" Kate whispered.

"No," Gabby said. "It's just the baby's room."

The girls lowered her back to the ground. "Let's keep looking," said Mia.

The next window they came to was open slightly. They could hear voices inside. "That sounds like Lizzie," Gabby said.

This time when the girls lifted her up, she saw Lizzie's room. Lizzie was sitting on her bed, with her back to the window. She was leaning forward, as if she was talking to something, but Gabby couldn't see what—or who.

Then Lizzie shifted and Gabby saw a faint circle of light on the bed, like a reverse shadow. It was a fairy's glow!

"Spinner's there!" she whispered.

"Are you sure? Did you see him?" Mia asked as they lowered her.

Gabby nodded. "I saw his glow."

"So Lizzie *did* take him!" Kate narrowed her eyes. "That little sneak!"

"Listen!" Lainey said suddenly, holding up a hand to quiet Kate. "Spinner's telling a story."

Through the open window, they could hear the sparrow man's voice. "The Clumsies who write books got the story all wrong. Thumbelina was a fairy, though that wasn't her name. Her real name was Maya."

"I thought Thumbelina was a girl," Lizzie said. "A teeny little girl."

They heard Spinner laugh. "Have you ever heard of a human girl as tiny as that? Now stop interrupting and listen."

"I have a plan for the rescue," Kate whispered. "As soon as Lizzie leaves the room, we'll boost Gabby inside and—"

"Shh, not yet, Kate," Gabby said. She moved closer to the window. "I want to hear the story."

"Maya was a fairy, almost like any other," Spinner began. "The only difference was, she was born without wings. But Maya didn't mind too much. She liked being close to the ground. She made friends with the tiny animals that lived in the earth. She loved being barefoot in the dirt and walking among the flowers."

As he spoke, Gabby seemed to feel herself shrinking. The hedge now loomed above her, high as the trees in a forest. She was no taller than a blade of grass.

Spinner went on. "One day, Maya wandered too far from home. She grew tired and fell asleep in a little flower. But a Clumsy woman came along and picked the flower and took it back to her house. When she discovered the tiny fairy inside, the woman decided to keep her. The flower was hers, she reasoned, so the fairy inside must belong to her, too.

"The woman was kind to the fairy—or thought she was, anyway. She sewed her clothes from scraps of silk and made her a bed from a walnut shell. She gave her a new name, too—Thumbelina."

Gabby looked down and saw that she was wearing an old-fashioned dress. It had a full skirt and tiny glass beads for buttons. Before her sat half a walnut shell, polished to a shine. There was a bit of wool for a pillow. When she climbed inside the shell, she found it made a snug little bed.

"But Maya was unhappy," Spinner continued. "She longed to be free again and to play among the flowers. Then one day, she met a toad who agreed to help her escape. . . ."

Spinner's words faded. Gabby found herself leaping through a night-dark garden on the back of a toad. The toad's skin was moist and she struggled to hold on.

But she clung to him with all her might, her heart beating wildly in her chest for fear that the Clumsy woman would wake up and find her gone.

When they reached a stream, the toad placed her on a lily pad. Three golden fish swam up and gently nudged her out into the current. As the sun rose, Gabby found herself drifting downstream on her lily-pad boat, watching butterflies as big as she was dart in the air above her.

When the lily pad became stuck on a rock, she begged for help from a flying beetle, who carried her to shore. Later, she took shelter from a storm in a mouse's hole and befriended a sparrow. At every turn, little animals helped her on her way.

All through the journey, Gabby knew

she was Gabby. Yet she saw the world through the fairy Maya's eyes. A mud puddle became a huge lake. A single raindrop soaked her to the skin. A patch of grass was a dense jungle.

Then one day, as Gabby the fairy soared through the air on her sparrow friend's back, she looked down and saw a field of flowers. Fairies darted among them, their glows twinkling.

"Maya knew she was finally home," Spinner said. "And that's the end of the story."

Gabby blinked. She was sitting on the ground outside Lizzie's window. Next to her, Kate, Mia, and Lainey looked as if they'd just awakened from a dream.

From inside they heard Lizzie say, "I was a fairy. I was right there in the story!"

Gabby smiled to herself. So Lizzie had also been carried away by Spinner's magic.

"I liked some parts," Lizzie went on. "But it was scary, too. I didn't like it when that lady took me to her house and I couldn't get home."

"Sort of like when you took me?" Spinner asked.

Lizzie was quiet for a moment. Then she said, "I just wanted to have my own fairy. I didn't think it would matter. I thought Gabby could just go get another one from that pixie place."

"Pixie Hollow," said Spinner.

"Yeah, Pixie Hollow." Lizzie sniffled, and Gabby thought maybe she was crying. "But now I don't know what to do. I can't give you back because Gabby will know

I took you and she'll be mad at me."

"No, I won't!" cried Gabby, popping up.

"Gabby, shh!" Mia, Kate, and Lainey hissed in unison.

But it was too late. Lizzie had heard them. She came over to the window and looked out. "Gabby? Why are you in the bushes?"

"Great," Kate groaned. "There goes my rescue plan." She put her hands on her hips and barked, "Listen up, Lizzie. Hand over Spinner, or else."

Lizzie's eyes went round. Gabby could see she was a little scared. "It's okay," she told Lizzie. "Kate's not really mean."

"Yes, I am," said Kate, trying to scowl.

"Just come outside," Mia said to Lizzie. "I think we can work this all out."

Moments later, the girls stood on Lizzie's front steps. Spinner was safely perched on Gabby's shoulder. And Glorinda was back in Lizzie's arms.

"It wasn't very nice that you took Spinner and didn't tell me," Gabby said to Lizzie.

"I know," Lizzie said. "And it wasn't very nice that you spied on me. So I guess we're Even Steven."

"Okay," said Gabby. "See you later, then."

She turned and went down the steps. Maybe Mia was right, Gabby thought. Maybe she shouldn't play with Lizzie. But then there would be no more fairy picnics at recess, or talking at lunch. And she wouldn't have a school friend who liked fairies as much as she did.

Gabby turned around and went back up the steps. "We can be Even Steven if you want," she said to Lizzie. "But I think I'd rather be friends."

"Me too," said Lizzie, and held out her hand.

As they shook on it, Gabby heard Spinner sigh in her ear. "What's the matter?" she asked him.

"Nothing," Spinner said. "I just like happy endings."

Chapter 10

"And that," said Spinner, "is the end of the story."

He was sitting on a toadstool in the Home Tree's courtyard, back in Pixie Hollow. On the ground at his feet sat a circle of fairies, listening. A healing-talent fairy stood behind him, gently straightening Spinner's bent wing.

"That was one of your best stories yet, Spinner," said Iridessa.

"Tell the part again about the Clumsy book," Beck said. "That was my favorite part."

"You mean 'Thumbelina'? The girl a toad wanted to marry?" Spinner asked.

All the fairies rolled with laughter. "Oh, oh!" Beck gasped. "Whoever heard of such a ridiculous story?"

From the direction of Havendish Stream, they heard more laughter—not the bell-like laughter of fairies, but the giggles of girls. A second later, Kate, Mia, Lainey, and Gabby came into view, climbing up the stream bank. Spinner was glad to see that Gabby had her wings on again. She was carrying a piece of paper in one hand.

"We're back!" Kate cried, throwing her

arms wide and tipping her face to the sun. "I *missed* Pixie Hollow!"

Lainey grinned. "You'd think we'd been gone for a year instead of just one day."

"It *feels* like a year when you're sitting at a desk all day long," Kate said. Spinner smiled. He knew what Kate meant.

"How was the second day of school?" he asked Gabby.

"Fun!" Gabby said. "Ms. Jesser gave us all classroom jobs—I'm the line leader. And at recess Lizzie and I played Red Rover with a bunch of other kids."

Mia shook her head. "I can't believe you still want to play with Lizzie, after everything that happened."

"I told you," Gabby said. "I like Lizzie. Anyway, I'd rather have a friend than a not-friend."

"Lizzie isn't so bad," Spinner agreed.

"Oh, I almost forgot," Gabby said. "Ms. Jesser handed these back." She held up the paper she was carrying. Spinner saw that it was the drawing they'd made together in class.

"What are the two gold stars at the top?" he asked.

"That means Ms. Jesser really liked it," Gabby said, beaming. "One gold star for each of us. You can keep it, if you want."

Spinner placed the paper on the ground, and the other fairies gathered around to admire it.

"I guess that means you're an honorary first grader," Gabby told him.

"Well, I'll be jammed and jellied," Spinner said in a soft voice. Then he blushed so hard his glow turned pink.

"Spinner has been telling us about his adventure on the first day of school," Beck said to the girls. "But it isn't really all true, is it?" She turned back to Spinner. "You didn't really battle a giant lizard in Gabby's classroom. Or get fairy-napped by red-eyed bandits. Did you?"

Spinner looked at Gabby and winked. "That depends on how you look at it," he told Beck. "What do *you* think?"

Read this Sneak peek of A Fairy's Gift, a Special Never Girls adventure!

Whenever she came to Never Land, Lainey found herself looking up at the sky. It was a remarkable color, a deep robin's-egg blue, and there was always something interesting to see. A flock of flamingos, maybe, or one of the Lost Boys flying by on his way to their hideout.

Today was no different. A swallow darted past. Lainey glimpsed a fairy with a long brown braid riding on its back.

"Fawn!" Lainey called, recognizing her animal-talent fairy friend. She thought she heard Fawn shout something in reply. But a second later, the bird disappeared into the trees.

Lainey turned to her friends. "I'm going to find Fawn and see if she wants to have a deer race. Want to come?"

Kate shook her head. "I want to go flying."

"I'm going to the meadow," said Mia.

Gabby waved her envelope. "I have to give out my cards."

Lainey nodded. "Meet you in a while." The friends always went to Never Land together—they'd made a rule never to go without one another. But once there, they often followed their own hearts' desires.

Kate headed to the mill, where she'd get

a pinch of fairy dust so she could fly. Mia strolled toward the meadow, where the prettiest flowers grew. And Gabby started for the Home Tree.

Lainey crossed the stream, heading toward the trees where Fawn had disappeared. As she walked, she whistled a Christmas carol.

Deck the halls with boughs of holly . . .

Lainey stopped. Was it her imagination? Or was there an echo?

She whistled again. A throaty chirp came back, matching her note for note.

Lainey scanned the trees. Since she'd started spending time in Pixie Hollow, her eyes had become much sharper. Now she spied a plump gray bird sitting on a branch. Could that be the one chirping?

She whistled another line of the song.

The bird peered at her with beady black eyes. Then it spread its wings and flew away. Lainey sighed. Had it only been her imagination?

She started walking again—and the forest around her burst into birdsong. In a chorus of trills, whistles, and cheeps, dozens of birds sang the song back to her.

As suddenly as they'd begun, the birds fell silent. Lainey had the feeling they were waiting.

Heart pounding, she whistled the next part. *Fa-la-la-la-la-la-la-la-la.*

The branches above exploded into song. Lainey's heart soared. She felt like a conductor with a great feathered orchestra. Lainey and the birds finished the song together.

"Bravo!" shouted a tiny voice. Fawn darted out from her hiding place behind a branch.

Lainey laughed. "Did you tell the birds to copy me?" she asked.

"So what if I did?" Fawn said with an impish grin. "It sounded wonderful. You're a natural song leader. Can you do any others?"

"You bet I can," Lainey said. She began to whistle "Jingle Bells," and the entire bird chorus followed along.

*

Gabby had been all over Pixie Hollow, delivering Christmas cards to her best fairy friends. She'd left two in a robin's nest for the animal-talent fairies Fawn and

Beck. She'd dropped one inside a buttercup for the garden fairy Rosetta, and another into Iridessa's favorite pool of sunlight. She left a card in the water fairy Silvermist's birch-leaf canoe. She placed one in a spiderweb hammock for Spinner, the story-telling sparrow man, and another on the knothole doorstep of Prilla, the fairy who'd first brought Gabby to Never Land. And for Dulcie, the baking-talent fairy, she placed one in an empty chestnut shell right outside the kitchen door.

Gabby had only one card left to deliver. Tucked between the roots of the Home Tree was a little building made from an old metal teapot. Gabby squatted down and tapped on the metal door.

She heard grumbling inside. Too late, Gabby remembered that Tinker Bell didn't like to be bothered in her workshop. She was about to leave the card on the pebble doorstep, when the door flew open. The tinkering fairy poked her tiny blond head out.

"What is it?" she asked, frowning.

"Nothing . . . I just . . . I have . . . This is for you," Gabby stammered. She held out the card.

As Tink took the square of folded paper, her face softened. On the front, Gabby had drawn a snowflake in silver crayon—silver because Tink liked metal things. Inside, the card read:

To Tink
Merry Krismus
From Gabby

"It's a Christmas card," Gabby explained.

Tink closed the card, then opened it and read it again. She looked pleased. "No one's ever given me a card before."

"Never?" Gabby was shocked. "What about for your birthday?"

Tink laughed. The sound was clear and bright, like a tiny bell ringing. "Fairies don't have birthdays."

"But then how do you know how old you are?" Gabby asked.

"We don't get older," Tink explained. "We just . . . are. Until we aren't." She admired the card again. "I want to give you something, too."

Tink darted inside her workshop. She returned holding something shiny, which she placed in Gabby's hand. It was a silver bell about the size of a gumdrop.

"It's a fairy bell," Tink explained. "Long ago, Clumsies hung them on their houses. It was a way of saying that they were friendly to fairies and magic."

Gabby rang the bell, which gave a high, merry jingle. She thought it sounded just like Tink's laugh.

"Of course, things have changed," Tink went on. "No one uses the bells anymore. I've kept some just because they're pretty."

Gabby rang the bell again, enjoying the sound. "It's a nice present," she said, putting it in her pocket. "Thank you very much."

"It's nothing," Tink said, waving off Gabby's thanks. "I'd better get back to work. I have an idea for a self-ladling soup pot. Haven't worked out all the kinks yet, though." She pointed to her pom-pom slippers. They were splattered with soup.

Tink went back into her workshop and closed the door. Before Gabby left, she peeked through the window. Tink was sitting in a chair made from a bent teaspoon. She was reading her card again.

*

Mia sat at the edge of the meadow, drowsing among the flowers. She knew her friends were off having adventures. *In a minute, I'll go find them,* she told herself. But the air was so soft, the flowers so bright and lovely, the little fairy doors and windows in the trees so charming, she just had to stop and soak it all in. Sometimes Pixie Hollow seemed exactly like a dream. A magnificent dream that Mia and her friends could return to again and again.

She'd been sitting for some time when she suddenly noticed a freckle-faced fairy in a green beanie perched on a nearby daisy. "Oh, Prilla!" Mia said, startled. "I didn't see you there. Why didn't you say something?"

"I'm just back from a blink," Prilla said. Mia noticed the fairy had the dazed look she got when she blinked her eyes and went to the mainland. Prilla always visited children on her blinks. That was how she'd met Mia, Gabby, and their friends— she'd accidentally brought them back to Pixie Hollow with her on a blink.

"Why do you do that?" Mia asked. "Go on blinks, I mean."

"Because it's my talent and I love it," Prilla replied. "And because it helps all fairies."

"Helps them how?" Mia asked.

Prilla looked surprised. "Don't you know? Through belief, of course! I help children believe in magic. And in turn, children's belief is what keeps fairy magic alive." As she spoke, she drew a ring in the air, leaving a trail of sparkling fairy dust. "Like a circle, you see? Fairies call it the Ring of Belief."

Mia watched the ring of fairy dust slowly fade. She had always believed in fairies, for as long as she could remember. It had never dawned on her that her belief was important to *them.* "It must be a nice job, meeting kids all over the world," she said to Prilla.

"It is . . . usually," Prilla replied. Her brow furrowed, but she didn't say more.